Daddy

Danny

Jakey

Isabelle

Isabelle

Mommy

Charlie

Gabriel

Charlie

Daddy

Danny

Keira

Gabriel

Jakey

Isabelle

Danny

Dear Reader,

This book is special! The guide below will help you understand the symbols.

 = Turn to the next page.

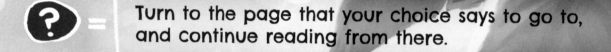 = Turn to the page that your choice says to go to, and continue reading from there.

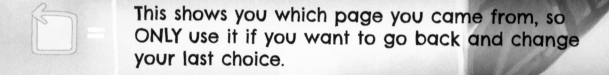 = This shows you which page you came from, so ONLY use it if you want to go back and change your last choice.

End #1 = You've reached one of the nine different endings! To reach another ending, start at the beginning and make different choices. Try to reach all nine!

- DANNY

What Should Danny DO?
On Vacation!

Ganit & Adir Levy
Illustrated by Mat Sadler

Hey! It's me, Danny! You probably already know that I'm a superhero in training, and that my most important superpower of all, is my POWER TO CHOOSE.

What you don't know is that I've been working on some cool new superpowers.

I can climb up walls.

I have night vision.

And I can kick like a ninja.
Hi-ya!

I'm so excited. Today is the day I've been waiting for. My family is finally going on vacation, and I want you to come with us! Ready? Let's go.

Woohoo! We're going to Paradise Springs Resort! They have an awesome water park, an arcade, and a kids club. And the coolest part is that my best friend Jakey will be there!

As soon as Daddy finishes loading the car, we hit the road.

A few minutes after we leave, I take out a Roboconverter.

"Aw, man! I forgot to bring a toy for the ride!" Charlie pouts. "Can we take turns sharing the one you brought?"

What Should DANNY Do?

Say no to Charlie? Go to page 12
Tell Charlie that he'll give it to him when he's done playing? Go to page 20

"OK," I say. Though I'm not so sure I can do this.

We start climbing the steps. Will they ever end? This slide is as tall as a T-Rex, but I take it one step at a time.

We get to the top and Jakey doesn't seem scared at all.

It's my turn to go and my hands are all sweaty. I can hear my heart beat really loud. I slowly sit down on the tube and wait at the top of the slide. I look over my shoulder. Lots of kids have lined up for their turns.

I take a deep breath and turn on my super bravery.
I push myself forward and...

"WHOOOOOAAAA!"

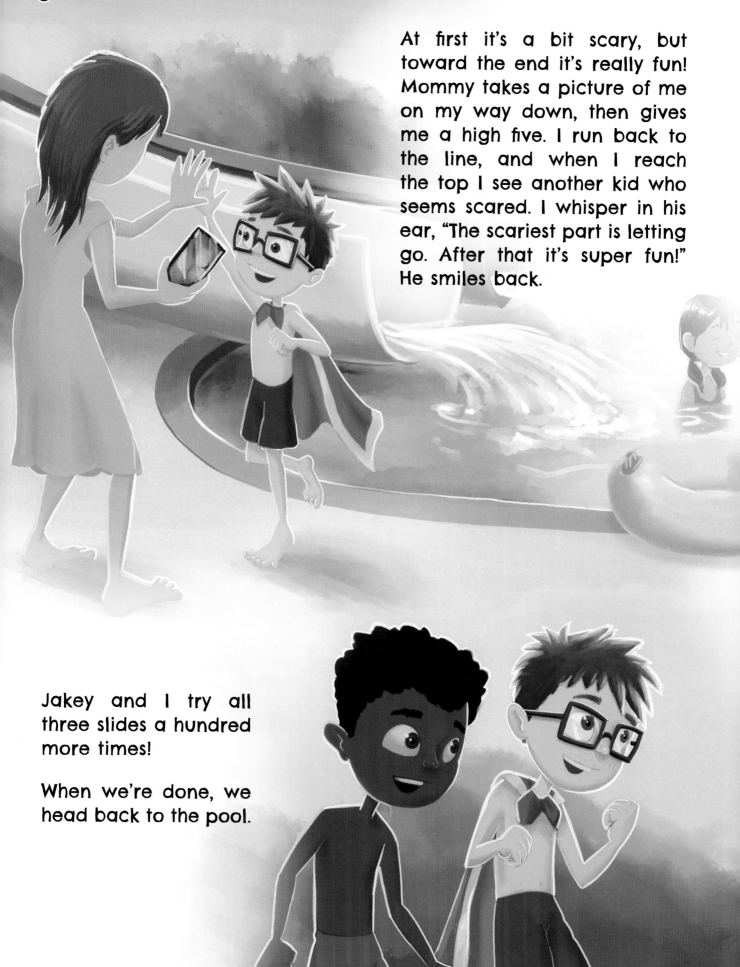

8

At first it's a bit scary, but toward the end it's really fun! Mommy takes a picture of me on my way down, then gives me a high five. I run back to the line, and when I reach the top I see another kid who seems scared. I whisper in his ear, "The scariest part is letting go. After that it's super fun!" He smiles back.

Jakey and I try all three slides a hundred more times!

When we're done, we head back to the pool.

"Hey, boys!" Daddy says. "It's time to hydrate. Let's go to the drink station and get some water."

"OK," Jakey says. "After that can we go to the kids club?"

"Sounds good," Daddy says. "I hear they have a huge obstacle course and a rock climbing wall you boys will love."

"Awesome!" Jakey and I yell.

At the drink station, Daddy and Jakey get their water and I'm next. Oh, cool! They have lemonade! I know I didn't pay for it, but I think it'll charge my superpowers better than water can.

What Should DANNY Do?

Fill his cup with water? Go to page 70
Fill his cup with lemonade? Go to page 68

"No way," I say. "You shoulda brought a toy for yourself."

The ride takes FOREVER. Charlie keeps kicking my foot and putting his arm on my chair. I keep shoving his arm off but it isn't helping. After a while I get bored and put the Roboconverter away. Charlie's reading a joke book and cracking up.

"Can I read some jokes?" I ask him.

"You didn't share with me, so why should I share with you?" he says.

After a million miles, we finally get to Paradise Springs Resort. Daddy and Mommy ask us to wait on the couch until we're checked in. I sit as far away from Charlie as possible.

I look towards the arcade and see Jakey there. I'm so excited that I run straight over.

"Hey, Jakey!" I yell.

"Hey, Danny!" he says. "I can't believe that we're both here together!"

"Yeah, I'm so happy I finally got here," I say.

"Want to play a round of air hockey?" he asks.

"You're on!"

We zoom to the air hockey table. Jakey scans his arcade card, and we play a game. When we finish, Jakey says, "Hey, want to win some tickets so we can get some prizes?"

"Great idea!" I say.

I check my pockets and realize I don't have any money. I have to go get some from Mommy.

I run back to the lobby, but I don't see her. I look for Daddy at the counter, and he's not there either. Charlie is gone, too.

Uh-oh. I look everywhere, but I don't see them. Where'd they go?

What Should DANNY Do?

Go look for them? Go to page 44
Stay calm and ask a safe helper for help? Go to page 28

Isabelle sees the boy with the cool cape, red hair and blue glasses look in her direction. She hopes he will stop and play with her, but he just keeps walking.

She throws the frisbee across the play area a few more times, but gets tired of chasing after it by herself.

At dinner, Isabelle's dad asks her if she is enjoying their vacation.

"It's been OK," she says. "I wish I had someone to play with. Everyone stares at me, but why don't they want to play with me?"

"Oh, sweetie," he says. "They're just not used to seeing kids in wheelchairs. If they knew how kind, funny, and incredible you are, they'd all want to play with you."

He wipes her tears away.

"Hey, I hear they're making s'mores and playing a movie by the pool," he says. "Would you like to go?"

"Yeah!"

They finish dinner and head to the pool.

"Thank you so much for taking me on this vacation," Isabelle says. "You're my best friend."

He smiles and gives her a hug. "I love you so much, Isabelle."

"I love you too, Daddy."

End
#8

I come up with a plan.

"Mommy," I say. "I'm so sorry, but I just broke Charlie's water gun. I want to buy him a new one."

"Wow, Danny," she says. "I'm so proud of you for taking responsibility for your actions. Do you have the money to buy one for him?"

"Not yet, but I'll save up until I can afford it."

Just then, Charlie comes back from the slide. "Hey! Who broke my water gun?!"

"I'm so sorry, but it was me," I tell him. "I promise to buy you a new one really soon."

"But I was just about to play with it!" he yells.

"Here. You can play with mine for the rest of the trip." I hand him my water gun.

He calms down. "Thanks," he says.

We jump in the pool and take on Dr. Ninjario together. Since Charlie has my gun, I get creative and come up with a new way to get the bad guys.

This day started out pretty rough, but I know that if I use my POWER TO CHOOSE wisely, the day can only get better from here.

End
#9

"Sure, you can play with it when I'm done," I say.

"Thanks!" Charlie says. He takes out a joke book to read while he's waiting. That looks fun too! We take turns playing with the Roboconverter and telling each other jokes. We laugh and have fun the whole trip.

"Five minutes till we get there!" Daddy exclaims.

Wow, that drive went by so fast!

We get to Paradise Springs Resort and wait in the lobby while Daddy checks in.

Charlie and I start a no-laugh challenge. Charlie tells me the first joke:

"What do you call a dinosaur that is sleeping?" he asks. *Hmmm*, I wonder.

"A Dino-Snore!" he yells.

I imagine a dinosaur snoring, and I can't help myself—I start cracking up!

Neither of us can stop laughing, so we just agree to laugh as hard as we can!

Just as Daddy finishes checking in, we see Jakey and his family at the arcade.

"Hey, Mommy! Can we please, please go to the arcade?" I ask. "Jakey is there!"

"Sure," Mommy says.

I use my super speed to zoom over to Jakey as Mommy gets me an arcade card.

"Hey, Jakey!" I say.

He runs over and gives me a high five!

We shoot baskets, bowl, and fire at targets to get as many tickets as we can.

When we're done, we each turn in our tickets to get a hand clapper, a chocolate bar, a slimy snake, and a top secret disguise. I wonder if Mommy will recognize me.

"Wanna meet my family at the Wonky Water Zone after lunch?" Jakey asks.

"Yeah!" I say. "Let me ask my parents if I can."

They say yes, so right after lunch, we all meet Jakey's family at the pool.

We apply our sunscreen, then Jakey heads toward the humongous slide.

"Come on, Danny," he says.

"Uh, maybe I'll catch up later," I say. But that slide looks super scary. I'm not so sure I want to try it.

I play by myself for a while, then Jakey comes running back.

"Hey, what are you doing here?" he asks. "This is the funnest slide ever! Let's go now before the line gets too long."

What Should DANNY Do?

Go down the slide with Jakey? Go to page 6
Tell Jakey the slide looks scary? Go to page 90

Oh, no! My family is gone. But where did they go? Why did they leave me?

I get scared and start looking around, but then I remember what Mommy taught me. If I ever get lost I should stay where I am and yell out for my parents. If they don't answer I should ask a safe helper to help me.

A safe helper is another mom with kids, a security guard, or a person who works at the place I'm lost.

"Mommy!" I yell. No one answers, so I yell again, but I still don't see her.

Then I see a mom walk by with her son.

"Excuse me," I say. "I think I'm lost. Can you help me find my family?"

"Of course," she says. "Do you know your mommy's phone number?"

"Yes." We call Mommy together and she says she'll come right away.

A minute later, I see Mommy running into the lobby. I'm so relieved.

"Danny!" She gives me the biggest hug, and thanks the woman for helping me.

"I was so scared you guys left me. I'm really sorry I walked off."

"We'd never leave you, Danny," she says. "I'm so proud that you did exactly what we taught you to do when you get lost, but I hope this was a good lesson to never wander off alone."

After lunch, we meet Jakey and his family at the pool.

He hands me a waterproof walkie-talkie that he brought.

"Let's see how far apart these work," I say. I zoom to the other end of the pool.

"Can you hear me?" I say into the walkie-talkie.

"Yeah, I hear you. 10-4."

I go even further, "Can you hear me now?"

"Danny, there seems to be a situation by the towel stand on my side of the pool. Come quick!" Jakey says.

I use my super speed to zoom back. I see lots of kids laughing and pointing at a boy. It looks like his swim trunks fell off!

"Isn't that hilarious?" a boy asks me.

What Should DANNY Do?

Laugh with the rest of the kids? Go to page 40
Tell the kids to stop laughing, and help the boy? Go to page 56

Oh, no! Charlie is going to be so upset. I have to think fast. I grab the water gun and drop it behind the bushes.

Just then, Charlie comes back. "Hey, where's my water gun?"

"I don't know," I quickly respond.

He looks for it under the lounge chair and in the trash. My tummy doesn't feel so good.

49

Just then, a girl comes up to me with Charlie's broken water gun in her hands. "Hey, I saw you playing with this earlier." She hands it to me. "I found it behind the bushes."

Charlie sees that it's broken. He looks really mad. *Uh-oh.*

He storms at me and pushes me towards the pool. Before I fall in, I grab his arm and pull him with me. We wrestle in the pool until the lifeguard jumps in to separate us.

"Didn't you hear my whistle?" he asks. "What are you kids doing?"

Mommy hears the ruckus and comes over. Everyone is staring at us.

"Let's head back to the room," she says. "You boys need to calm down again."

In the elevator, I ask what floor we're on.

"18," Mommy responds.

Charlie quickly presses the button before I get to it.

"No fair," I yell. "I wanted to push it!"

We get to the room, and Daddy says that we'll be staying in and having peanut butter and jelly for dinner.

"What?" I say. "I wanted to go out for dinner, and peanut butter and jelly doesn't charge my superpowers!"

"Sorry," he says. "I think we all need to relax a bit."

I go to sit by the TV, but then a great idea pops into my head. *Hmmm... What if I call room service and order some chicken nuggets for dinner?*

What Should DANNY Do?

Eat the peanut butter and jelly sandwich? Go to page 66
Order chicken nuggets? Go to page 60

I laugh with the rest of the kids and the boy starts crying.

33

Suddenly, laughing feels wrong.

The lifeguard hands the boy a towel and we all start walking away.

Jakey and I want to keep testing out the walkie-talkies.

"Let's see if they're really waterproof," I suggest.

"Cool idea," Jakey says.

I use my super speed and run to the pool, but right before I'm about to jump in, I slip and fall on my tush. "OWW!" I yell.

I look around and see that kids are laughing at me.

I zoom back to Mommy and ask her if she can take me up to our room.

"Why, Danny?" she asks.

"My tummy doesn't feel good," I say.

Later, Mommy sits next to me and says, "Sometimes our tummies feel funny when we're worried. Did anything happen at the pool that made you feel uncomfortable?"

I think about it and realize she's right. "I fell and everyone laughed at me," I tell her.

"I bet that didn't feel too good," she says.

It sure didn't. Then I think about the boy whose bathing suit slipped off. It was really wrong of me to laugh at him. I wonder if his tummy hurt, too. Next time I see kids laughing at someone I'll make sure to use my POWER TO CHOOSE wisely and stand up for what's right.

End
#4

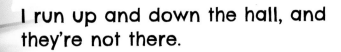

I run up and down the hall, and they're not there.

I run back through the arcade, and the lobby. They're not there either! Oh, no!

What if they left me here alone?

I run to the restaurant and look through all the tables. I see a door. Maybe they went in there?

I run through the door and end up in the kitchen.

"Hey, you can't be in here!" a man yells.

I run out and start to cry. I've been alone for sooooo long. Where did they go? Why did they leave me?

After a hundred thousand minutes, a woman from the hotel walks up to me.

"What's wrong?" she asks.

"I can't find my parents," I say.

"Don't worry, sweetie, I'm sure we can find them."

She asks me for my full name and speaks into her walkie-talkie.

A few minutes later, I hear someone announce on the loudspeaker, "Can the Miller family please come down to the lobby? Miller family to the lobby."

Soon after, I see my family running towards me. "Daddy!" I yell.

"We found you!" he says. "We were looking for you everywhere."

I squeeze him really tight.

"Danny, you can't wander off like that," he says. "It's not safe. And if you ever get lost, you have to remember what we taught you. Stay where you are and call out for us. If we don't answer, you need to ask a safe helper for help."

"Oh yeah," I say. "A safe helper is a mom with kids, a security guard or a person who works at the place where I'm lost."

"That's right," Daddy says.

We go hang out in our room while we all calm down.

After lunch, we head out to the pool. Charlie runs off to go down the slide. I play with my water gun, but after a while I need more fire power to get Dr. Ninjario and his cronies. I grab Charlie's water gun, and it's fully loaded. Now I can shoot at them with two guns at once!

I jump in and out of the pool to get away from the bad guys, but then, oops! Charlie's gun falls and breaks.

What Should DANNY Do?

Take responsibility for breaking Charlie's gun? Go to page 18
Hide Charlie's gun before he comes back? Go to page 34

"Cool frisbee!" I tell her.

"Thanks!" the girl smiles. "It can fly super far."

"Nice. Wanna play catch?" I ask.

"Sure!" she says.

"My name is Danny. What's yours?"

"Isabelle but my friends call me Izzy."

We play catch, and she's really good.

"You've got a really strong arm," I tell her.

"Yeah, my arms are strong because I need to push myself around a lot," she says.

"Cool," I say.

We play for a while, and then she asks, "Wanna hear a funny joke?"

"Yeah."

"Do you have any holes in your shorts?"

I look at my shorts. "No," I say, confused.

"So how do you put your legs through?"

We both laugh.

We tell each other joke after joke and laugh so hard our stomachs hurt. She knows way more jokes than I do.

"Hey, my brother and I have a cool joke book. Wanna check it out?" I ask.

"Sure!" she says. She asks her dad if she can come, and he says yes.

We head back to the pool, and I see Jakey and Charlie.

"This is my new friend, Izzy," I tell them. "She's super funny!"

"Nice to meet you," Jakey says.

Just as I hand her our joke book, Mommy comes over and tells us that it's time for dinner.

Izzy's dad says, "I was planning on bringing Izzy back in an hour for s'mores and a movie by the pool. Would you like to join us?"

"That would be great," Mommy says.

"Yay!" we all cheer.

We come back after dinner and Izzy tells me she loves my cape. I offer to let her wear it.

As soon as I put it on her, she does the coolest spin moves, and the cape flies through the air.

Her dad comes to me and says, "Thanks for making her day. I wish there were more kids as nice as you."

I smile and say, "She made my day, too."

We roast marshmallows by the pool and watch the movie on the big screen. Turns out Izzy lives a few miles away from me. We make plans for an ultimate frisbee playdate next week! Score!

This has been such an awesome day!

End #3

I think fast. I use my super speed to grab a towel and hand it to him.

"Hey!" I yell to everyone. "How would you feel if this happened to you?"

The kids stop laughing and walk away.

"Thanks," the boy says.

"You're welcome."

Jakey hands the boy his swim trunks. He hurries to the bathroom to put them back on.

The lifeguard comes up to Jakey and me and says, "What you just did took courage. You didn't give in to peer pressure and helped a boy in need. That showed real leadership."

"Thanks!" we say.

After a while, it's super hot by the pool so I think of the best way to cool down.

"Hey, Mommy, can we get some ice cream?"

"That sounds fun," she says.

Score! We head to the ice cream shop.

"What flavor will you get?" I ask Jakey.

"Rainbow sherbet all the way!" he says. "What about you?"

"Cookies and cream!" I say. My mouth starts watering just thinking about it!

We get to the ice cream shop, but there's a sign on the door that says, "Closed for Remodeling."

"Aw, man!" I say. "Why does ice cream need remodeling? I like it just the way it is."

What Should DANNY Do?

Ask his mom if they can get ice cream another time? Go to page 88
Yell because he didn't get ice cream? Go to page 76

I pick up the phone and hit the button for room service. I'm pretty hungry, so I think I'll want ten nuggets all for myself.

"Room service. How can I help you?" a lady asks.

I change my voice to sound like an adult as best I can. "Uhhh, can I get, uhhh, ten chicken nuggets please?"

"Sure, ten orders of chicken nuggets," she says. "Anything else?"

"Uhhh, yeah. Barbecue sauce. Lots of barbecue sauce," I say. "And a Shirley Temple with a cherry on top."

 "OK, you got it. Coming right up to Room 1876 in ten minutes," she says.

Everyone sits on the balcony to eat their peanut butter and jelly sandwiches. Then we hear a knock on the door.

"I'll get it," I say.

"OK," Daddy says. "But make sure to check who it is first."

I rush to get it so I can sneak the chicken nuggets in without anyone noticing.

But when I open the door, I see a whole cart with plates and plates full of chicken nuggets! *Whoa!*

The man rolls the cart into the room.

"Thank you," I say as he leaves.

I only meant to order ten pieces, but they sent me ten plates! What if I get caught?

I think fast and roll the cart into the bathroom. I move all the plates into the bathtub. Wow, this is a lot of chicken nuggets! Maybe I can have some for breakfast tomorrow. I put the last plate in the tub, grab the Shirley Temple and jump in. Just before I put the first nugget in my mouth...

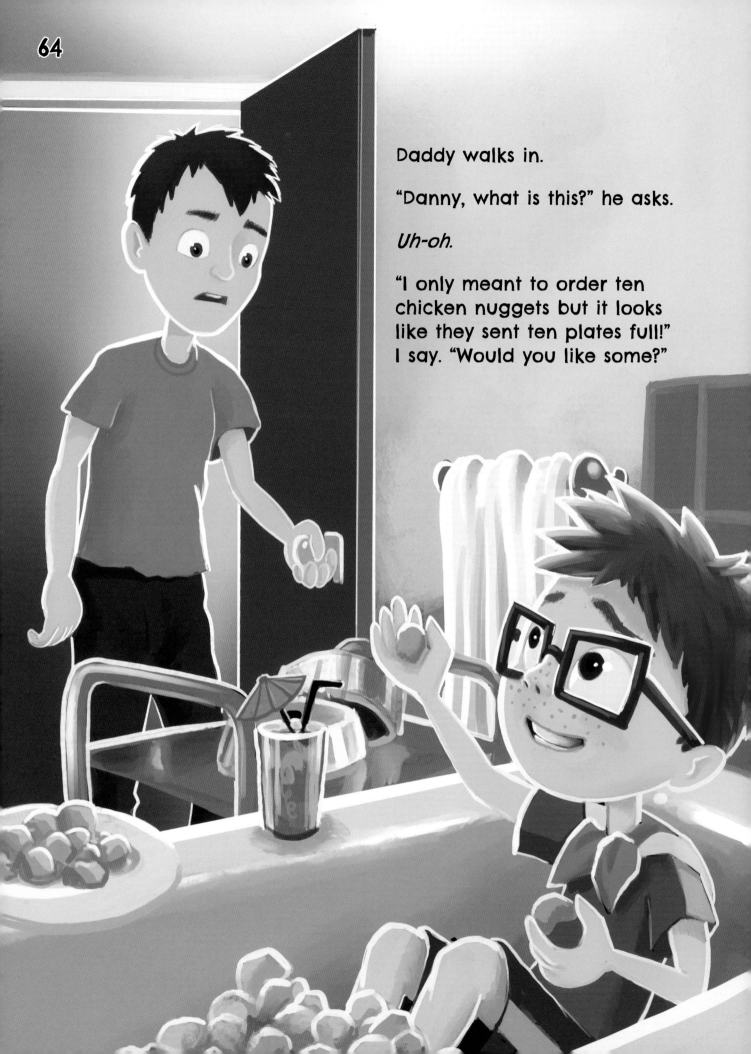

Daddy walks in.

"Danny, what is this?" he asks.

Uh-oh.

"I only meant to order ten chicken nuggets but it looks like they sent ten plates full!" I say. "Would you like some?"

"I think you know better than to order room service without permission, Danny."

My face turns red. This day is definitely not going well.

"I know that going on vacation is exciting, so I was willing to forgive some of your behavior from earlier in the day," he says. "But I will expect for you to pay for these chicken nuggets." He picks up the receipt. "Looks like they cost a little over a hundred dollars."

"A hundred dollars!?!" Oh, no! This has been the worst vacation ever! And now I'll need to sell a LOT of lemonade to make that much money!

End #2

I offer to help Mommy spread the peanut butter. We all go sit on the balcony to eat our sandwiches.

"I know today didn't go quite as planned," Daddy says, "but I think with some good choices, we can have a much better day tomorrow."

Charlie and I agree.

"How about we grab some popcorn and watch a movie tonight?" Mommy suggests.

"That sounds fun!" I say.

"If I make better choices, can I go to the arcade and the Wonky Water Zone with Jakey tomorrow?" I ask.

"Sounds like a plan," Mommy says. "I'll call his mom after the movie."

"Thanks," I say. "I know tomorrow will be a much better day if I use my POWER TO CHOOSE wisely."

End #5

68

I need to see if this lemonade is as yummy as the lemonade I make at home.

I fill my cup, then gulp it down so fast that I start to cough! Lemonade squirts out of my mouth and nose! *Eeww!* Daddy comes to see what's wrong.

"You OK, Danny?" he asks.

"Yeah," I say, but I'm still coughing.

11

"Hey, that's gross!" Jakey says. "Your water is yellow!"

Daddy looks at my cup and understands what I did.

"Jakey," he says, "maybe you should head back to your parents by the pool. I need to have a talk with Danny."

Aw, man! I was so excited about the kids club! Jakey goes to his parents, and Daddy pulls me aside so that no one hears.

"Danny, you can't take something you didn't pay for. That's called stealing. I think you already know better than that."

My face turns red.

"I can tell you're feeling bad," he says. "Let's make this right. How about you pay for the lemonade with your own money?"

He hands me some money, and I promise to pay him back from my allowance.

I stand in line and tell the man what happened.

"Oh, that's nice of you to do the right thing," he says. "That'll be $4.00."

Four dollars?! I only charge 50 cents at my lemonade stands. That was one expensive mistake!

Daddy and I head towards the pool area.

DRINKS

Lemonade

Go to page 92

I fill my cup with water and chug it down. Mmmm, this water is so refreshing, I can feel it charging my superpowers all over my body!

When I'm done with the water, I start munching on the ice chips, and then a great idea pops into my head.

"Hey, Jakey. Want some ice down your back to cool down real fast?" I ask.

"Yeah, sounds fun!" he says.

I take out a piece of ice and put it down the back of his shirt.

"Ooooo!" he yells as he laughs. "That's freezing!" He takes out a piece of ice and puts it down my shirt.

We laugh the whole way to the kids club with ice melting down our backs. One piece even gets in my shorts!

KIDS CLUB

WELCOME TO KIDS CLUB

We check in and get our glow-in-the-dark wristbands. Score! They're starting a new race in five minutes! Jakey and I join as a team, and the counselor shows us the map.

Then he says the winning team gets free ice cream sundaes!

"We can do this, Jakey!" I say.

"We'd better," he says. "It looks super fun, and I want that sundae!"

Daddy leaves, and we go straight to the obstacle course.

Whoa! It looks amazing!

START

We line up. On your mark, get set, go! The race starts out super close, but three teams fall out during the obstacles over the water.

Jakey tags me for the final leg of the race, and it's just me and a boy from the yellow team left! He's a little ahead of me, so I turn on my super speed. I'm about to catch up, but then I see him trip over one of the kids on the sideline. He falls to the ground and looks hurt.

What Should DANNY Do?

Finish the race? Go to page 86
Help the boy up? Go to page 80

"No fair!" I yell. "You said we could get ice cream!"

"I'm sorry, Danny," Mommy says. "I didn't know the shop was closed."

"But you promised!" I yell. "This stinks!"

"I know you really wanted ice cream, Danny," she says. "It must be upsetting to think you're going to get a treat and then not get it. Maybe we can find a different treat?"

"No way!" I yell. "I only want cookies and cream ice cream, nothing else!"

"Let's go relax by the pool," she says.

"I can't relax!" I yell. "I want my ice cream now!" I kick the trash can next to me but my super muscles are too strong. The trash can falls over and some of the trash spills out!

Aw, man! Now I have to pick up the trash,
and I don't get ice cream.

Mommy calls Jakey's parents to come get him, and he goes back to the pool.

As we head up to the room, Mommy wants to talk. "Danny, I'm surprised by how you used your POWER TO CHOOSE just now."

I think about the way I reacted, and I know she's right. Maybe I'd still be having fun with Jakey if I used my POWER TO CHOOSE wisely.

End #6

I really want to win the race, but if he's hurt, I think I should help him first.

I help him up, and he smiles. We walk together to the finish line, and we break the ribbon at the same time!

The counselor comes over and says "It's a tie! The red team and yellow team both get ice cream sundaes!"

All the kids cheer!

Then she says, "But we also have a sportsmanship medal to give out! We only give this out to someone who goes above and beyond by treating their competitors fairly. This medal goes to Danny Miller on the red team!"

She gives me the medal, and Jakey comes over to give me a high-five.

Just before we get our sundaes, I see the boy who fell during the race.

"Hey, I'm Gabriel. Thanks for helping me during the race," he says.

"My name is Danny, and I'm happy to see you're feeling better," I tell him.

We all talk for a while, and I learn that Gabriel and I have so much in common! His favorite show is Ninjitsu Ninja just like mine, and he also loves to skateboard!

"Hey, do you and Jakey want to come hang out at the wave pool tonight?" he asks. "There'll be a glow zone party!"

"Sounds awesome!" I say.

We ask our parents, and they agree, so after dinner we head to the wave pool.

Whoa! The glow zone party is like a carnival! The music is awesome, and the games are super fun! They even have a churro station. Score! This is the best vacation ever! I can't wait to see how tomorrow goes if I continue using my POWER TO CHOOSE wisely.

End #1

I zoom past the boy and finish the race! I win! I go to give Jakey a high five, but he's going to help the boy up.

While we're waiting to get our ice cream sundaes, I see the boy who fell, and he looks sad. I know I'd be sad if I fell and lost the race.

"Hi, I'm Danny. Are you OK?" I ask him.

"Yeah," he says. "My name is Gabriel."

"The race was really close. You might have won if you hadn't tripped," I say.

"Thanks," he says.

The counselor brings out our ice cream sundaes, and I know just what to do. I ask Jakey, and he agrees.

"Can you please split our sundaes into two?" I ask. "I think Gabriel and his teammate deserve some ice cream, too."

The counselor looks at me and smiles as she leaves. When she comes back, she brings out four full sundaes! They're dee-licious!

"Hey, do you guys want to come hang out at the wave pool tonight?" Gabriel asks. "There'll be a glow zone party!"

"Sounds awesome!" I say.

Go to page 84

CLOSED
FOR
REMODELING

"It's OK, Mommy," I say. "Maybe we can get ice cream another time."

Mommy smiles. "That's such a mature response, Danny. I'm so proud of you."

We head back to the pool, and after a while it's time for dinner.

"I know this day started out a bit rough," Mommy says, "but since then you've made the best of it by making great choices. How about we invite Jakey's family out to dinner with us?"

"Yesss!!!" I yell. I run over to tell Jakey. He's super excited, too.

We both order chicken nuggets and Shirley Temples. They're delicious!

After we finish eating, the waiter brings out the dessert menu. Woohoo! They have ice cream!

"Can we puh-lease have some ice cream?" I ask.

"Of course!" Mommy says. "I'm so happy you'll get your ice cream after all."

This day didn't start out so great, but I'm proud I used my POWER TO CHOOSE wisely to turn it around.

End #7

"Ummmm, I think I'm going to stay... because... that slide looks scary."

"OK, see you later," he says as he zooms back to the slide.

I look for Charlie, but he's busy playing with Keira, Jakey's sister.

I guess I have to play by myself. I practice my handstands and water flips, but after a gallon of water goes up my nose, I need something else to do.

I get out of the pool and look around.

I see a jungle gym and tell Daddy I want to check it out. When I get there, I see a girl in a wheelchair with a frisbee in her hand. I love playing frisbee.

I overhear her talking to her dad. "I'm so bored," she says. "I have no one to play with."

What Should DANNY Do?

Continue playing by himself? Go to page 16
Ask the girl if she wants to play with him? Go to page 50

About the Authors

Ganit, a former teacher, and Adir, an astrophysics junkie, are parents to four amazing kids who love learning about how to use their POWER TO CHOOSE wisely.

About the Illustrator

Mat Sadler is an Illustrator of things. He lives with his wife and two kids in England (but he doesn't sound like Hugh Grant–or Pierce Brosnan for that matter. He's from Essex).

Danny

Meet (the real) Danny, the authors' adorable nephew, who served as inspiration for the main character. He's a real superhero in training who never misbehaves. 😉

 @ganitandadir

Charlie

Jakey

Daddy

Charlie

Mommy

Danny

Danny

Mommy

Isabelle

Gabriel

Jakey

Charlie

Dear Parents & Educators,

Children enjoy the book best, and learn the most, when reading through multiple versions of the story. Because this may be your child's first exposure to a story in this format, you may need to encourage them to make different choices "just to see what happens."

Through repetition and discussion, your child will be empowered with the understanding that their choices will shape their days, and ultimately their lives, into what they will be.

Ganit & Adir

Text and Illustrations copyright © 2020 by Ganit Levy & Adir Levy
All rights reserved. Published by Elon Books, LLC P.O. Box 35263, Los Angeles, CA 90035
No part of this book may be reproduced or transmitted in any form or by any means, electronic or mechanical , including photocopying, recording, or by any information storage and retrieval system, without the permission of the publisher.
What Should Danny Do? On Vacation / by Ganit & Adir Levy.

Summary: Danny, a superhero in training, learns the importance
of making good choices while on vacation (post corona lockdowns).
Levy, Ganit & Adir, authors
Sadler, Mat, illustrator
Morales, Elaine, additional artwork and formatting
ISBN 9781733094689
Visit www.whatshoulddannydo.com
Printed in the United States of America
Reinforced binding
Second Edition, April 2021
10 9 8 7 6 5 4 3 2 1